Calendiles

All things considered; Jenny didn't mind
being a vampire

Shena Wheeler/ Rupert Mcintosh

pencil

ISBN 978-93-5667-136-2
© Shena Wheeler/ Rupert Mcintosh 2022
Published in India 2022 by Pencil

Contributors:
Illustrator: Cerenaty Reyes
Illustrator: Shena Wheeler/ Rupert Mcintosh

A brand of
One Point Six Technologies Pvt. Ltd.
123, Building J2, Shram Seva Premises,
Wadala Truck Terminal, Wadala (E)
Mumbai 400037, Maharashtra, INDIA
E connect@thepencilapp.com
W www.thepencilapp.com

DISCLAIMER: *This is a work of fiction. Names, characters, places, events and incidents are the products of the author's imagination. The opinions expressed in this book do not seek to reflect the views of the Publisher.*

Author biography

Shena and City Of are two further books written by Shena Wheeler or Rupert Mcintosh. For more information about upcoming fanfiction, books, novels, and graphic novels, follow Shena on Twitter at @Calendiles_T. Shena was born in Stratton, Penslevania. Shena currently resides in Cookeville, Tennessee.

DISCLAIMER: *This is a work of fiction. Names, characters, places, events and incidents are the products of the author's imagination. The opinions expressed in this book do not seek to reflect the views of the Publisher.*

Author biography

Shena and City Of are two further books written by Shena Wheeler or Rupert Mcintosh. For more information about upcoming fanfiction, books, novels, and graphic novels, follow Shena on Twitter at @Calendiles_T. Shena was born in Stratton, Penslevania. Shena currently resides in Cookeville, Tennessee.

CONTENTS

Slice of Life

All things considered, Jenny didn't mind being a vampire. Sure, her diet now consisted of scraps from the butcher's shop, her taste in clothes had taken a severe turn into recreating The Cranberries at every opportunity, and her online occult consultation business was a slow start, but it was better than the alternative. which was just a slight case of "Angelus deciding to snap her neck just to prove how worthless she was." His last-second decision to turn her so she could torment the Scoobies was a blessing. It just took months—and the discovery of a yellow disk by a promising red-headed witch—to get there.

Jenny took a swig of her pig's blood from her mug as she curled into herself on the couch, continuing to monitor the extreme lack of hits her occult web page was getting.

"Come on, how is this not picking up globally, let alone in Sunnydale?" "She?" she said to herself with frustration as she clicked refresh again."

She had half a mind to reach out to her family in Romania to see if they had a need for a technopagan— enshrouded—a vampire with a mind for demons and a heart of gold. But she knew better than to contact a family that had nothing to do with her.

She thought to herself, "Not much of a family then, I guess."

Jenny couldn't help but stare at the stream of light entering the living room through a skylight in the ceiling. It cascaded across the living room throughout the day as the sun moved, and currently, it cast a bright beam just behind the back of the couch. When Jenny moved in with Giles after she got her bearings post—soul restoration, Giles offered to cover it up permanently. She remembered him saying that an architectural choice was not worth her safety. She immediately declined his offer. Sometimes when he wasn't here, she'd walk right up to the beam of light. She'd stick her hand out, close enough where her fingers were almost bathed in sunlight, and then retract at the last second. It was nice to have the illusion of normalcy.

Jenny slammed the lid of her laptop in defeat. She held her head in her left hand as she leaned on the back of the couch and let out a long sigh. She never thought she'd get to the point where she missed teaching, especially at Sunnydale High School. When she was there, she always thought of it as a cruel haunted house—a place where book-steeling vampires, zombie football players, and a particularly rat-faced principal lurked in the shadows. Seven months out of work and having to spend it all in literal shadows had changed her mind. All she could think about was having an entire classroom of students eager (well, at least willing) to learn about computers; a library that captured the awe-inspiring of a west coast sunset; and plenty of broom closets in which to drag a certain librarian into stolen moments of bliss when no one was looking.

She closed her eyes as she remembered the feeling of Rupert's lips on her neck, of him pressing her against the utility shelves, of him whispering his adoration for her as his fingers crept slowly down-

Jenny frustratedly and rather haphazardly discarded her laptop on the coffee room table with a thud.

She thought it was no use thinking about what we almost did or what we couldn't do now.

Just then, she heard a key unlock the deadbolt of the front door. It opened with urgency as a slightly frantic tweed-clad figure entered the living room.

"Jenny?!" His voice erupted with haste as his briefcase was all but forgotten on the floor near the door. He made a beeline towards the couch where he sat. "I heard a rather loud crash. Is everything alright? "

Giles rushed to sit down next to Jenny on the couch and brought his hand to her cheek. It had been 7 months since Jenny had been turned, almost 4 since she had gotten her soul back, yet Rupert still flocked to her as quickly as he could when he sensed there was something wrong. Maybe he thought his attentiveness to her could somehow prevent what's already happened to her. Jenny liked to believe it could.

"I'm fine, Rupert," She said convincingly as she leaned in to greet him with a kiss. Whether or not she was trying to convince him or herself, she didn't dwell on it.

"My web pace isn't getting as much traffic as I hoped it would," she leaned into his touch.

Well, it's fairly new to start a business on the web, yes? Maybe it just needs more time," Giles continued to caress her cheek as he looked at her lovingly.

"I guess," Jenny responded skeptically. I mean, it's been a month and suddenly the call for occult help is no more? No one needs an online prayer circle! Nary a bone needs to be cast!" Jenny started to get off the couch when Giles put a hand on her knee to hold her down. They both knew she had more than enough strength to overpower him. It wasn't unnoticed by Giles when she sat back down.

"Darling, it's been a slow summer." I feel it would be thoughtless to fail to be grateful for such events given that Buffy has only just returned from Los Ang-LA. However, if there is one thing living on the Hellmouth has taught me, it's that danger is only just around the corner. I'm sure you'll be getting, er, more traffic soon. "

Jenny leaned her head closer to Rupert and said with a grin, "Are you trying to make me feel better by promising me that there's going to be a bunch of vampires and demons trying to kill us sometime soon?"

He returned a toothy grin as he stroked her hair, "Precisely." At least I have a girlfriend who I know can more than handle any threat coming our way.

"Are you asking me to protect you?" How forward-thinking of you, "Jenny began to lean in."

"What can I say?" Rupert replied softly as he began to meet her lips, "My girlfriend knows how to take charge." And then he was kissing her.

Jenny let herself enjoy the illusion for as long as she could. They've had to develop strict rules on how far they could actually go before they had to stop. It was one thing to enjoy physical intimacy; it was another to allow passion to take over at the cost of her soul.

As her lips moved against him, she moved her hand onto his thigh and the other into his hair as she let her fingers play with his silky strands. He moaned as his hand fell to her waist and pulled her close as he continued to kiss her. She licked his lips and sighed as he opened his mouth to let her tongue slip inside.

Screw it, she thought, it's been a crappy day.

She moved to straddle him on the couch, his hands sliding across her thighs. She leaned down and whispered in a sultry voice she could barely recognize as her own, "This okay?" She was inches away from his face, looking deep into his eyes.

"Oh, yes," he gasped, holding her cheek as he reclaimed her mouth with his. He knew they would have to stop soon. This always built too fast between them. A fall out of passion never realized. A quick kiss before heading to work would turn into desperate necking against the front door, and Giles was seriously flirting with the idea of asking Willow to keep the soul restoration handy for last-minute requests. He knew it was an impossible situation. He was unable to consummate a relationship with his live-in girlfriend, a woman he was hopelessly in love with. The only thing more impossible was the thought of letting her go.

Jenny began to grind on Rupert's lap as she sucked a bruise into his neck and snapped him back into the moment. He had removed his hands from her thighs and managed to get out a slightly painful, "Moloch," before he had even realized he'd said it. They thought a mutually agreed upon code word for stop might make things easier. Giles didn't know if it did, but he would hate to see how this situation could get much more difficult.

Jenny immediately stilled and leaned up, looking at him with guilt.

"I'm… sorry," she gasped, lifting herself off of Rupert's lap and back onto the couch.

He immediately reached for her hands.

"You have nothing to be sorry for, love," Rupert spoke softly, albeit out of breath, kissing her knuckles gently. "All

things considered, it's a wonderful way to be
greeted upon coming home."

Jenny let out an exacerbated laugh. "Yeah, just another
reminder about how I can't be what you deserve."

That's when Giles froze. He immediately pulled her hands
to his chest, just over his heart, and looked deeply into her
eyes.

"Being with you is more than anything I could ever
deserve." I love you."

Jenny's resolve softened

She believed him.

"I love you too, England."

Giles reached in for a gentle kiss. Just as Jenny could feel
herself wanting to push it further again, he released her lips
and rose from the couch.

"How about I start dinner? Blood sausage, perhaps?" Giles
disappeared into the kitchen as Jenny stayed seated on the
couch, the same frustration she had

before Rupert came home welling up inside her.

Maybe Jenny minded being a vampire more than she
thought.

Getting Re-ensouled

Getting re-ensouled is not as romantic as it sounds. It's actually quite painful.

Not as painful as losing your soul, but still.

With Spike having kidnapped the unconscious Drusilla and Buffy and Angelus fighting in front of a still-inactivated Acathla, a vampire with Jenny's face observed the scene.

Well, this is boring, she thought to herself. Jenny wasn't very interested in ending the world. Sure, the thought of the balance between good and evil tipping toward demons sounded fun in theory, but she was more interested in seeing Angelus' vision realized. Human Jenny would have done anything to reign in Angelus' terror of evil. Vamp Jenny was much more interested in extending his destruction as far as possible.

Family loyalty always drives Jenny Calendar

However, while Angelus is preoccupied with his little girlfriend, Jenny, she finds herself some free time. Maybe it was time she had fun on her own before the Earth went tumbling into hell.

"Oh, Rupert! "Looks like I'm not quite finished with you," she mockingly sang as she sauntered towards the back of the mansion.

She took in the sight of him as she leaned in the doorway. Rupert Giles was in bad shape. He was doubled over in a chair, hands bound behind his back, shirt partly ripped open, with blood and sweat dripping from his head and fingers. His breath was shallow, but it was there. She was impressed.

She thought to herself with pleasure, Who knew the old librarian had stamina? Jenny honestly didn't know how much more he could take, but she grinned thinking of how entertaining it would be to find out.

Sensing her presence, Giles slowly lifted his head.

"What more do you want from me?" Giles managed to whisper in defeat.

"Oh, don't worry, babe," Jenny spoke slowly as he tried to focus his eyes on her. "None of us have much time left."

"Well, good." He breathed out as he let his head fall back, trying to readjust himself against his restraints as best he could. "I'm not overly fond of your company."

"Oh, England. That hurts my feelings, "Jenny faked a pout as she slowly stepped into the room. "That's no way to speak to a lover." She kneeled down next to him and ran her hand up his open shirt, across his face, and through his hair. She whispered in his ear, her lips brushing his skin. Well, I guess we weren't lovers, but we were close, weren't we?" She placed a soft kiss on his ear.

Giles knew it wasn't her. It couldn't be. His Jenny was dead. He had been reminding himself of such since the moment he woke up in the mansion. He knew he needed to be strong and resist the urge to believe he could have her back, that they could be together. But he had already failed to remember that earlier, Jenny had told him how Angelus could awaken Acathla. What does it matter now? The Earth was doomed regardless. Why not give in to the illusion?

Giles lifted his head and tried his best to focus. Even with the room spinning, he could make out her brown eyes against the dark room.

"I wanted so much for us. I wanted us to be lovers, to be together. I don't know how to push past this," he said with a dry throat, tears spilling from his eyes.

"Oh, Rupert, and you think you deserve that?" Jenny cocked her head, feigning interest, continuing to softly brush his hair with her fingers.
Giles closed his eyes. "No, but I had hoped-

Jenny roughly grabbed his hair and pulled his head back. He cried back in anguish as she leaned in closer, her lips brushing his cheek.

"Oh, you had hoped?" "What a useless feeling for you to have," she spoke with venom as she sneered at him.

"There's no hope for you, for me, for us," She grabbed his hair tighter. His breathing sped up as he cried in pain.

With his neck completely bare and exposed, Jenny thought having one last drink with the pathetic man in front of her was the perfect way to welcome hell on Earth.

"Look at me," she commanded slowly. Giles managed to fight against the pain and pry his lids open.
He looked in horror as he saw his beloved Jenny in vamp mode.

"We'll never be together; not after what you did to me."

Jenny opened her mouth and began to bite down on Giles' neck when she heard a clatter behind her. She quickly turned around, but before she could investigate, Xander Harris was already in mid-swing with a baseball bat speeding toward her face.

"God, there are so many other teachers I would have rather done that to," she heard the boy say to himself as she regained her composure on the floor. By
the time Jenny was able to get to her feet, Xander had already finished untying the knots around Giles's hands and feet.

"You know what, Xander, I've had it up to here with your immature bullshit," she said as she drew closer to the boy

who was supporting the barely conscious Giles. "It's time-
"

Suddenly, Jenny froze as she felt something clawing itself through her body. It felt foreign, ugly, and cloying; it felt like something had been deep within her, locked away, and was finally emerging. It was fighting to break free of the cage it had been confined to. It felt as though it was spreading through her veins, contaminating every part of her body, slowly taking over her last bit of control—it felt like something good.

"Oh my god," Xander said to himself as he looked at her with wide eyes, still trying to keep a fading Giles awake and conscious. Jenny threw her head back and her arms out as a beam of light went through her.

"Giles, hey, Giles, stay with me, you're going to want to see this," Xander said as he gently shook the man. Giles managed to look up just in time to see Jenny re-ensouled. Jenny was discussing the events of that evening, and Giles recalled knowing he was out of it. Hours of torture and dehydration do that to a man. But he does remember the last thought he had before blacking out was wondering if it was possible that Willow could do such a foolish thing. Giles grabbed Jenny's hand as he told her he was desperately thankful she had.

Xander wasn't quite sure he could believe what he just saw, but he was pretty sure he just saw his best friend re-ensoul their favorite teacher right in front of
his eyes. He thought about how before he had left the

hospital, he had convinced Willow to re-ensoul Ms. Calendar before she tried with Angel. He told her it was because Buffy could handle Angelus, but they weren't sure if Giles would be able to take on vamp Jenny. But Xander knew it was because he wanted Angelus to die. A better chance of Ms. Calendar getting her soul back was a happy bonus.

"What is going on," Jenny managed to get out between gasps, attempting to regain her breathing and steady herself back onto her feet. "Where the hell am I?"

Xander quickly shifted Giles in his arms so he could walk over and lean down toward Jenny.

"Ms. Calendar," he said with panicked confidence, "We've got to go now." He quickly grabbed her arm to pull her up, and helped to carry both her and Giles out of the mansion. As the group stumbled past Buffy and Angelus—now fighting in front of a fully awakened Acathla—Xander wondered if he had made the right choice in advising Willow. He decided that having Ms. Calendar was worth it, and vowed to never think of it again.

Jenny remembered the panic of not being able to form a linear timeline of events in her memory. Last she remembered, Angelus had her in his grip at the school, his teeth in her neck, draining her life. She was now huddled on the ground with an anxious Xander and a clearly very inured Giles outside Angelus's mansion. Her focus was on trying to remember how she had gotten there and vanished as she realized Rupert didn't appear awake. She scurried to his side.

"Rupert, baby?" Jenny said, panicked and hurriedly, kneeling next to Rupert, holding his face, willing him to look at her. He didn't make a sound.

Jenny was about to start shaking him when the memories started to resurface….Jenny laughed with Angelus as he recounted the story of love letters in the library…waiting for Giles at his apartment the night they were to reconcile, only to reveal her true vampiric form when he leaned to kiss her…torturing Giles for hours only earlier that evening…

Jenny immediately threw herself back onto the ground, propping her body up with her arms behind her, frantically trying to catch her breath.

"No, no, no, please no," she sobbed, looking up at Xander, pleading with him to make this make sense. to be able to explain what was happening without confirming what she already knew to be true. that she was a vampire.

The last thing she remembered before passing out for the night was Xander rather unconvincingly whispering, "Ms. Calendar, it's okay. It's going to be okay. Trust me, this is all going to work out…

What Do You Want

They have been fighting more lately.

Not about big things. The big things they had a decent grasp on. For instance, Jenny was the first to admit that she had difficulty parsing out the difference between her partner being annoyed with her behavior and total character assassination. An annoyed Rupert asking her to remember to please sign off the internet so that their phone line wasn't constantly unavailable somehow felt like he was saying she was The Most Inconsiderate Person to Walk the Earth. Once Jenny realized that her boyfriend could think the world of her and also be annoyed that she never did the dishes because they "needed to soak", their relationship seemed to even out.

For a time.

It appears that anything now sets the other off. Rupert didn't heat her pig's blood enough? They argued until they didn't speak to each other for an entire weekend. Jenny left a slew of diskettes on the coffee table. Rupert spent all night on the couch. They both seemed to be aware of the absurdity of their situation, yet they both seemed wildly incapable of fixing it

Luckily, today seemed like it was going to be a good day.

Jenny's legs were lazily strewn across his lap. Giles was sitting on the couch wearing a casual sweater and jeans. His eyes crinkled with laughter as he stroked her legs. Jenny's head was thrown back in laughter as well.

"You cannot be serious, Jenny!" Giles managed to get out between chuckles.

"I swear!" Jenny crossed her heart and held her hand up in honor. She reached for her wine on the table as her laughter subsided. Although she missed the taste of such delicacies as McDonald's and In-and-Out, she was grateful vampires could still enjoy booze.

"I walked right up to my headmaster, clad only in my bra and underwear, and said, in the most mature voice that I could muster at 17, 'You bet your ass that I started that protest! "Girls should be able to wear pants as part of our uniform if they want!" He honestly did not know what to say!" Jenny's story was punctuated with laughter from Giles as he listened to his girlfriend's indecorous and quite brilliant adolescent behavior.

"He must have quickly given into your demands, dear," Giles let out as he wiped away a tear from his eye, still chuckling softly to himself.

"Oh god no! He immediately called my Uncle Enjoys and had me taken home for the semester. "God, that was an awful winter," she recalled as she took another sip of her wine. These Saturday afternoons, stolen hours away spent with each other, relaxed, together on the couch, really did make up for the evenings of petty fights they seemed to be getting into more often lately.

Misplaced tension, Jenny thought to herself as she finished off her glass and reached for the bottle to pour what she had dubbed a "movie pour" worth of wine.

Giles said with ease, "Yes, well, knowing your family, I cannot imagine they were too forgiving," as he finished his glass and took the bottle from Jenny's hand, ready to empty it.

Jenny felt the prick of an insult. She recoiled her legs up to her chest and pushed herself up so she was sitting more erect.

"Well, I was a kid, so of course they were understanding," Jenny spoke candidly, not trying very hard to hide her annoyance.

Giles could sense her aggravation as he paused and took a moment to compose himself. When it came to Jenny's family, he knew to tread lightly. He knew the balance: be supportive of her disappointment and hurt with how they'd treated her since she became a vampire, but never actively criticize them. He may have stepped too far over the line.

Giles cleared his throat and tried to sound as civil as possible, "Quite right, as they should, I only meant -"

"I mean, that was a big deal for my family. Getting thrown out of boarding school? I can understand their frustration with me. " Jenny was becoming actively more agitated as she brushed the hair that escaped from her messy bun behind her ears.

"Darling, I did not mean any offense, I only meant -"

"I know what you meant. It would just be nice if I could tell a story about my family without you needing to take a jab at them. " Jenny had fully retreated into herself. She knelt up near her chin as she held her legs. Giles was desperate to salvage the day. He knew if he just apologized, and said he did not mean to insinuate any negativity towards her family, but to comment on the story, there was a chance for peace.

Frankly, he was tired of backtracking his disdain for how these people treated the love of his life.

He took a moment to compose himself. Then, decisively, he placed his wine glass down on the table.

"I'm sorry, Jenny, but I have yet to hear a single story about your family where they treat you with any kindness or respect, regardless of your age and circumstance. "It's difficult for me to empathize with those who always seem to hurt you so dearly," Giles looked down. He could not make eye contact with her. He knew saying that meant another fight, but he didn't regret it. Standing up for what he believed in, which in this case was the value of one

Jenny Calendar, was fundamentally more important.

He'd defend her. Come hell or high water.

Jenny was looking at him, eyes wide and her mouth agape. With a frustrated scoff, she set her wine glass on the coffee room table next to his and stood up. She walked around to the back of the couch, careful to avoid the afternoon beam of light filtering through the skylight onto the back of the couch and the floor beneath. Even being indoors, Jenny was reminded that she wasn't human.

"You know," she began, her head down, bracing herself with both hands on the back of the couch. "I appreciate you always looking out for me and having my back, but stuff with my family is wildly complicated." The same curse they used to torture the vampire who destroyed their legacy has been used upon one of their own, I don't expect them to suddenly be okay with me." She lifted her head, the exacerbation almost tangible.

"Jenny," Giles said, tentatively placing his glasses on the table as well, rubbing his eyes, wanting to get through his hands with as much ease as possible. He spoke softly.

"I know that, love. I just…I just think you deserve better. " He finally was able to look at her, and he started with soft eyes.

Jenny practically laughed.

"Better? I failed in every way possible with them! " She threw her hands up in frustration. She glanced down at the desk behind the couch. Adorned with a Tiffanys lamp and other ancient relics and mystical nick-knacks, the couch also held several unopened letters addressed to Jenny from her family. She hadn't been able to open any of them. So much for gaining super-human strength when you become a vampire

She leaned over, just avoiding the sunlight streaming through, to grab the latest parcel.

"And now, I won't even open the correspondence I get from them! It seems to me they have a whole lot to be upset over. " She held the small package, staring at it, willing it to give her the peace she so desperately needed.

That's when Giles rose and walked around the couch. He was almost flushed with her when he tried to take her hands. She quickly recoiled and held on tighter to the parcel. He held his breath and his hands momentarily in the air, hopelessly unsure as to what to do, and then landed them on her arms tentatively, lightly stroking them up and down, hoping to convey his affection.

"Love, opening that will do you no good."

Jenny didn't want to hear it. She didn't want to listen to someone else about what she should or shouldn't do. Listening to others putting their own desires above her own had led to a life where she had to avoid wooden T's and the California sun.

It was time to do what she wanted. Even if it meant facing the harsh reality, she wanted to pretend it wasn't real.

"No, no, let's see what the old family has to say, huh?" Jenny said, biting with sarcasm as she began to open her parcel. She dumped the contents into her hand to reveal a single piece of rolled parchment and a small pouch wrapped in old, gold fabric. It fits in the palm of Jenny's hand and felt as though it held some sort of liquid.

Giles moved his hands, wavering, and finally reached out to hold her hands, trying to convey the competing emotions he felt. He wanted to apologize for yet again causing another fight. He wanted to hold her because he knew how deeply her family's disdain for her grieved her. He wanted to kiss her full of promise, to show her how much he loved her. He wanted to whisper in her ear that he knew this situation was challenging, but that she was the greatest thing to ever happen to him.

He didn't know what he should do.

So he stammered, and held her hands, the parchment and pouch between their joined palms. He held her gaze, green eyes holding brown, and he let himself be honest.

"Darling, what could this possibly be? What could they possibly send you to make up for the absolute abuse they've put you through? What? What do you want?!"

Later, when recalling the incident, Giles couldn't remember exactly what he expected from this outburst. He remembers being satisfied that finally, and without an agenda, had asked her what she was hoping for from her family, but he certainly didn't expect what came next.

As soon as Giles finished his exclamation, he squeezed Jenny's hands in his, hoping to ground her, to keep her there at the moment with him, to prove to her that he did want her to answer the question. In between their hands, however, was still a yet-to-be-ascertained liquid-filled pouch. As soon as he squeezed their hands, the pouch broke, quickly releasing a green goo between their hands.

The sudden and unexpected mess broke the tension.

They separated as Giles looked at his hand in disgust, and Jenny looked in curiosity. It was quite vicious. What was more remarkable, though, was how bright it began to shine on Jenny's palm. As Giles began to wipe the substance away on his jeans, cursing to himself under his breath, Jenny watched in wonder as the green mixture seemed to dissolve into the flesh of her palm.

"Oh no," she said with familiar panic as she looked up into Giles' eyes pleadingly. She felt a painful shock shoot straight from her palm up through her arm and into her entire body. She would never forget the pain of having her soul forced back inside of her body. While this wasn't quite it, it also wasn't far off.

She immediately fell to her knees, clutching her hands into tight fists, and doubled over. Giles immediately met her on the floor, one hand on her hip and another on her head. He was gently stroking her hair, softly saying her name.

"Jenny, love, what is it?" He desperately searched her face for answers, willing her to be alright.

Suddenly, her head shot up towards the sky, her mouth agape. Giles fell back as a bright light deep within Jenny boiled up, projecting itself through her entire body, and beamed out of her face. Just as it burned white hot, it exited her body.

She fell back, panting heavily, trying to catch her breath. It was not a familiar feeling.

As she regained control over her body, she began to gasp desperately, licking her lips, trying to regulate her breathing. She felt as though she would never be able to stop breathing so quickly.

Giles was still on his knees in front of her, out of breath himself. He held his hands out, hovering around her, attempting to protect her from any additional foreign element in their immediate vicinity.

That's when his eyes drifted and he noticed where her left hand had landed on the floor to catch herself. He was petrified.

"Jenny..." He spoke delicately, almost afraid.

She was still trying to calm the spinning. One moment, she had been fighting with Rupert - which was the last thing she wanted to be doing with him - and the next, it felt as though she was almost passing out from a lack of oxygen, felt as though there was a rhythm in her chest, a drum beating with a cadence that sparked life. She knew of course-

"Jenny…"

She thought she could hear Rupert saying her name between thoughts, but she couldn't quite parse out the sound. She was about at capacity, experiencing sensory overload when-

"Jenny!"

She was able to focus, zoom in on Rupert's face, and hone in on his soft green eyes. She followed his gaze which was focused down unto her left hand, which was stabling herself on the floor.

In the direct beam of light from the Saturday afternoon sun bursting through the skylight.

Jenny looked upon her hand in disbelief as it continued to not burst into flames. As she attempted to catch her breath and feel the pace of the thump in her chest slow, she felt the warm rays heat her hand. She had no idea how. She had no idea why. But she knew in her gut what was happening.

She looked back up at Rupert and immediately recognized the gears turning.

"What's happened?" She said between gasps, trying to stay as objective as possible. There was no way this was happening. She needed Rupert to ground her back to reality which was never this kind.

He began to think out loud in shock. "Green viscous liquid, you were dead, you're breathing now, and you're able to survive in sunlight," he brought his hand up to check her pulse, to confirm what he already knew to be true. "I think…I think the pouch contained the blood of a Mohra demon, which means…"

"I'm alive." She finished for him.

"Yes."

Jenny knew that they needed to think. To take time and ascertain what had happened given the dramatics of the last several minutes. They needed to confirm their theory. That she was alive with no chance of losing her soul. They needed to be absolutely sure before they did anything crass.

However.

Rupert Giles was a man of carefully calculated decisions. Putting the greater good above his own needs was his mode of operation. However, even given the absolute remote possibility he and Jenny could have a happy ending, even the slightest of chances, he'd call you a fool to expect he'd do anything other than going all in.

Rupert moved his hand from her pulse to the back of her head and pulled her in for a hard kiss.

She immediately met his lips with equal passion, wrapping her arms around him, deepening the kiss, and feeling his pulse beneath her. He was alive. She was alive. He kissed her back, hungry, desperate to occupy the same space as her. Willing his body to mold to hers.

He was hers. That's all he ever wanted.

His other arm snaked behind her waist, pulling her to him as he carefully brought them both to their feet.

Waiting is for the dead, she thought.

"I want you; I need you, babe," she was able to whisper between kisses, her voice dripping with lust. This almost didn't feel real. Felt like a dream, the kind of dream she'd had a hundred times since she got her soul back. The kind of dream she hated to wake up from. But this was real. His hands were on her head and waist, grounding her, holding her down.

"I want you," Rupert managed to gasp as she began an assault on his neck, licking away the sweat. He closed his eyes and held her tight against him as he found the will to move them towards the stairs. He had to get them to their bed.

As soon as his feet hit the first stair, her hands moved down to the hem of his sweater and began to pull it up over his head. He wasn't thrilled with the idea of taking his hands off of her for any reason, but he quickly responded by removing his sweater and depositing it on the floor. As she held him to her by his waist, his hands found her cheeks as he held her head. They both were gasping for breath as they looked into each other's eyes. The intensity of the moment lent itself to the enjoyment of their absolute happiness as they began to smile, leaning their foreheads together.

"I love you," she said ardently.

He gazed down at her, drawn in completely. Nothing was ever this important.

"Jenny, I love you." Her soft laugh was met with one of his own as he recaptured her mouth with his. He held her to him as they clumsily made their way up the stairs, kissing. He reached for her t-shirt as she pulled it off with ease, dropping it to the floor below their loft with a smile.

Burning

It was bad enough knowing that his girlfriend, Jenny Calendar, had been turned into a vampire by the former paramour of his slayer, but it was another to have to deal with the demon wearing her face feigning love and affection for him.

This was the second time he'd returned home to find what appeared to be a love letter attached to his front door, this time with a single red rose. After a long day of work trying to come up with a plan to defeat Angelus, Spike, Drusilla, and Jenny—that is, the demon wearing Jenny's face—in addition to extra training with Buffy, this was beyond the last thing Giles wanted to be greeted with upon coming home. The letter, written on the same parchment Angelus had been using for his morbid drawings, was folded in half and hanging from the knocker on his door. As he slowly approached, he could identify the large, curvy "J" written on the outside of it as being in her exact handwriting. It was a perfect facsimile of how Jenny used to sign her notes to him. Whether it was a simple note left on his desk in the morning wishing him to have a good day or a slightly more suggestive one she'd sometimes deposit directly into his back pocket at school when no one was looking, she'd always sign it with the same chaotic and rounded letter.

After the truth about Jenny had come out and he was spending a typical evening at home, now alone, he wondered if she signed the letters with a simple "J" because it was her way of secretly displaying vulnerability and authenticity with him. Maybe the "J" was for Jenny, maybe for Janna, maybe for both. Either way, he'd never know now.

He'd always feel a rush of excitement and pure happiness when he saw that big, flowing "J." Now, it appeared cold and sinister on his door, illuminated by moonlight, mocking him. The sight made him sick. It was made worse knowing that the demon who put it there knew this would be the emotion elicited. It felt like a sick violation. Only he and Jenny should know about those notes and how she signed them, not some demon using those memories to torture him.

He quickly continued through the courtyard and yanked the rose off of the door, throwing it harshly into the bushes. He ripped the note off of the door, cursing under his breath, and locked himself inside his flat. Once he deposited his briefcase and coat on a chair to his right, he made a beeline for his decanter of scotch and poured a generous serving. He downed the burning liquid, closed his eyes, and clenched the glass. Once the pain subsided, he opened his eyes and stared down at the note in his hand. Anger was quickly turning into abject sorrow. He cursed himself for once again letting himself be fooled. His initial gut reaction to both the first and this second letter had been hopeful. He somehow knew that Jenny was alive and trying to get in touch with him. That's when common sense and logical thinking kicked in and he realized these were the taunts from a demon with her face and nothing more. He hated that he fell for it again. He was starting to believe that his feelings for Jenny and his complete loneliness at losing her were making him a bigger target than he realized. He reached for the decanter and poured himself another scotch before finding a seat on the couch.

The demon left the first note for Giles on the day after Jenny, and he was to reconcile. He had stopped by her classroom late the night before, and both of them were working well into the evening. She had indicated that she and Buffy had spoken and that the two women seemed to have reached an understanding – at least enough for Giles to feel a little guilt about attempting to rekindle his relationship with Jenny. She had something to possibly tell him and was going to come over to his place that night. He felt a glimmer of hope the entire drive home, the first spark of happiness he'd felt in weeks. He waited patiently in anticipation of her arrival for over 45 minutes. When she knocked on his door and he opened it, he could immediately sense something was amiss.

First, upon opening the door and seeing her face, he was able to discern something was slightly off about her. Given their fight and subsequent estrangement of the last few weeks, her smile and use of a pet name seemed too out of place as she seductively purred, "Hello, England." Second, she seemed to have gone home to change before coming to see him. That wasn't weird in and of itself necessarily, but what struck him was her outfit: she had put on a turtleneck. Giles knew she preferred open-collar tops, especially when they were not confined to the dress code of campus. It was odd to him that a dark turtleneck was the top she chose to wear for a late-night visit to his home.

Finally, when he stepped aside and opened the door enough to allow her to walk in, she didn't move. Instead, she spoke slowly, "Is this you inviting me in?" He paused to look at her with confusion. Why was she behaving so bizarrely?

"P-pardon?" He whispered, trying to gauge her meaning.

"Is this you, inviting me in, England? After everything the last few weeks, I want to make sure you know what you're doing. "If I come in, I don't plan on leaving until morning," she spoke surely, letting her eyes trail down his body and back up again.

Giles felt his heart rate pick up as his breathing came in slightly faster. As he continued to hold the door open, he fought every molecule of his body screaming to invite her in immediately, take her in his arms, and plan to just talk everything out in the morning. However, his training kicked in, and he hesitated. His stomach fell and he felt panic in his chest as he considered what the evidence was telling him.

"Jenny," he began carefully, speaking slowly and with purpose, "why are you trying to get me to verbally invite you into my home?"

"Why are you being so paranoid, Rupert?" She said, cocking her head with concern. "God, you need to lighten up." "I could help you with that," she said, her voice dripping with longing. Just tell me that's what you want and I'll do it. "I'll give you everything." She leaned into him, emphasizing the last few words. He noted she got as close as she could without actually crossing the threshold into his home.

At that moment, he knew. He felt her, no, not her, it. He felt it.

He knew the most strategic move would have been to play along. Either invite it in and wait for it to drop its guard before attacking, or simply attack it now in his courtyard. Anything where he could gain their trust and retain the element of surprise.

But he couldn't bear to think of a strategy. He was too busy trying to make sense of what happened. A million thoughts raced through his head at once. Jenny is dead, Jenny is a vampire. Angelus must have turned her. Jenny is dead. Jenny is gone. I just saw her alive an hour ago. I must stake her. I must stake it. I don't know if I can. Jenny is dead.

Hot tears welled up in his eyes, and he tightened his expression until it was stony and full of anger. He clenched his teeth and grasped the door until his knuckles were white.

"Damn," the demon said, looking down, shaking its head with a frustrated laugh. "I knew it was a long shot, but I was really hoping to kill you right before fucking you. I thought you were actually pathetic and lonely enough to invite me in. "No biggie, I won't underestimate you next time."

His heart sank, and he let out an audible gasp. Any foolish hope that he was just severely misreading her or that the situation was gone? She had been turned into a vampire.

Jenny Calendar was dead.

"Well, in that case, I'll plan to see you soon, Rupert. Oh, don't cry, love, "she said with mocking care, eyeing a tear falling down his stoic face. "I'll get you soon enough."

"I am going to kill you," Giles swore in a low voice through gritted teeth, maintaining aggressive eye contact and taking the time to speak each word with authority.

"We'll see about that," she said sweetly with a smile before quickly changing her face to vamp mode and snarling at him. Giles shuddered to witness the demon take over his beloved's face, and like a reflex, he took a step back into a fighting stance.

That is when the demon reverted back to Jenny's face and laughed, a perfect imitation of the real Jenny Calendar's laugh, the kind that would reveal itself late at night when she was over at his place and they were finishing dinner or doing the dishes or watching a movie.

"Be seeing you," it said sweetly

Giles watched in horror as the demon took off into the night, leaving him frozen, holding his front door open, tears silently streaming down his cheeks, attempting to process what had just happened.

The next day, he woke up to a note on his front door. Jenny's characteristic "J" sprawled on the outside of the folded piece of paper. Upon opening it, he began to read how the demon knew exactly how Jenny had been feeling the last few weeks. Ashamed, hurt, and lonely, she realized she was in love with him and that it was probably too late to fix things between them. He could make out the joy the demon took in reporting how miserable she had been the last few weeks of her life and took particular pleasure in how it was caused by none other than Rupert himself. When he got to the paragraph detailing what Jenny had been hoping for the night before, he couldn't bring himself to finish the letter. He scanned it, and phrases such as, "longing for forgiveness" and "fantasized about coming in your arms" popped out at him. Despite the nasty hangover wracking his body, he immediately crumbled the letter into a ball, threw it into the kitchen sink, and used a lighter to set it on fire. He watched the letter slowly burn with a steely expression.

Now, months later, Giles was sitting on his couch, scotch in one hand and a second letter from the demon in the other. He took a swig of the scotch and placed the glass on his coffee table with a loud clank. He removed his glasses and rubbed his face. He wasn't getting nearly enough sleep as it is and letters like this did not help.

He finally opened the paper, revealing a short note written in Jenny's exact handwriting.

My dearest Rupert,

I miss you, England. These last few months have been miserable without you. It was hard enough having to deal with the entire Scooby Gang, including you, ignoring me before, but now I've tried to reach out and you still won't give me the time of day? I'm hurt. But don't worry, love; the end is near. For you, for Buffy, for everyone.

I'll be seeing you soon, Rupert. Sooner than you think.

Love,
Your Jenny

Tears stung Giles' eyes as he placed the note on the coffee table and finished the scotch, willing himself to focus on the burning in his throat and not nausea in his stomach. Clenching his teeth, he wondered how long he could put up with this before hitting his breaking point. Just when he thought her torture was over and let himself feel safe again, this note appeared on his door. That was probably its goal, he thought, slowly allowing him to regain a sense of safety, letting enough time pass for him to begin the grieving process before ripping the carpet out from underneath him.

Angelus clearly showed this demon a thing or two about torturing former loved ones.

He thought about going out right now and hunting it. He knew he was in no state of mind to do such a thing. Not only was it nearing midnight and he was beginning to feel slightly drunk, he knew even on his best day he'd be no match for a demon wearing Jenny's face. For all of his pontificating to Buffy about neither of them having the luxury of being a slave to passion, he knew he'd never have it in him to kill a demon wearing Jenny Calendar's face.

He knew how pathetic that was. He failed at being a boyfriend, and now it was causing him to fail at being a watcher.

Giles took a deep breath. Dear Lord, Buffy is quite right. I need to take a "chill pill' or what have you? He was quick to immediately comfort Buffy and assuage her of the guilt she felt, blaming herself entirely for this whole ordeal. He reminded her that she loved Angel, Angel loved her, and that no one knew what would happen – not even Ms. Calendar. He thought he should maybe extend a measure of that same kindness to himself. even if he felt like he did not deserve it.

Regardless, he needed to call it a night. He had an early meeting with Doug Perren of the Sunnydale Natural History Museum the next morning about what was described to him as "a large stela" adorned with unusual inscriptions. He prayed it was nothing mystical-that was the last thing everyone needed with Angelus and Jen-the demon-wearing Jenny's face stepping up their harassment.

Giles took one last deep breath and grabbed the note, heading for the kitchen. Just like last time, he crumbled it into a ball, threw it in the sink, and lit a match, setting it on fire.

He watched the white parchment shrivel, fire dancing on the edges, consuming the letter. All hope for a happy ending burns alongside it, dissolving into black ash.

Sunday Morning

Now that she was a vampire, Jenny woke up around sundown, ready to get her day started about the time Rupert was getting home from work. Her new sleep schedule took some getting used to, but it did remind Jenny of her college days, so she tried her best to embrace it. This day, however, was not normal. It was the definition of an abnormal day. Most notably, she was thrilled to be waking up at dawn.

Rupert was unconscious and naked against her, his face buried in her neck and his arm draped across her torso. He shifted slightly to lie on his back, turning into his embrace. He exhaled deeply as he drew her closer to him. She closed her eyes and rested her head on his chest, feeling his breath return to a steady rhythm.

With Rupert so close, his heartbeat under her ear, his skin on her skin, his warmth enveloping her… She drew in a deep breath and felt her lungs expand with every passing moment. She held on to her breath as long as she could. She finally let it out, enjoying the sensation of her body requiring another. It was a reminder that this is real. She's alive.

Jenny moved her head to look up at her lover. His expression looked blank, completely free of worry, fast asleep.

Jenny thought to herself as she studied his face, "I don't think I've ever seen him this relaxed, this carefree." She chuckled to herself, "I still got it." She rose from the bed, carefully lifting her head and gently removing herself from his arms. Once on her feet, she stretched, enjoying the pops and creaks of her depreciation. She relished the sounds of her body preparing for the day ahead.

She quietly walked over to the wardrobe to grab one of Rupert's pajama tops. As she finished buttoning it and lifted her hair out of the shirt, she took in the room: their clothes from the previous evening were strewn haphazardly everywhere. She was particularly proud of how Rupert's briefs somehow made it to the top of their dresser.

Jenny carefully padded down the stairs and was greeted by a forgotten, joyous mess: the remnants of about six different restaurants' leftovers. She laughed to herself as she remembered the previous evening.

"Oh, oh, Chinese food. Oh my god, Chinese too! I would kill for an egg roll right now!" Jenny beamed from the couch, clad in Rupert's robe. She quickly turned the yellow pages back to "C" to see if any Chinese restaurants in Sunnydale were still delivering at 9 pm. She got up and walked over to Giles sitting at the bar near the phone donned only in a pair of sweatpants, gathering phone numbers onto a legal pad.

"Of course, dear, let's add it to the list. What does that make now? American, Italian, Mexican…," Giles wanted to be sure he had his girlfriend's entire order. Normally, he took pride in cooking his own meals, never sending for delivery or takeaway. But when your girlfriend who hasn't been able to eat real food in months suddenly has a human appetite again, you make her dinner wishes come true.

"Don't forget that ice cream place! I cannot wait to eat like, an entire pint of rocky road," Jenny took the pen from Giles' hands, leaned over his shoulder, and wrote down the number to the Chinese restaurant.

"It's the first number on the list," Giles said softly, leaning into her, and placing a warm kiss on her neck.

Jenny closed her eyes and sighed, "Well good," she turned her head and met him with a long kiss. As she pulled away and saw Rupert's eyes closed, the smile on his lips, she whispered, "Now hurry up and place these orders, so we can get back to…more important things." He listened.

Jenny shook her head at the memory with a smile as she slowly waded through the living room, a healthy number of to-go containers piled on the coffee table. She paused as she saw the skylight beaming the newly risen sun into the living room, light shining directly on the top of the back of the couch. She walked up to the beam, eyeing the floating particles of dust illuminated by the orange and red hues. She felt the warmth from the light as she reached out her hand, fingers inches from the beam. She held her breath as she reached directly into it.

Light on flesh. Not a whiff of smoke in sight. A huge smile crept on Jenny's face.

Enjoying the sun of a new day, Jenny didn't hear Rupert as he made his way downstairs. Eyeing Jenny twisting her wrist and curling her fingers in the sun, he made his way behind her, slipping his arms around her waist, careful not to tug her corkscrew dangling from her belly button.

"Good morning, love," he whispered in her ear nestling against her head. Jenny immediately responded, turning into his touch, feeling his bare chest on her back, and placing her hands on his as they rest on her stomach.

"Good morning to you," she said back as she craned her neck back to give him a slow kiss. Their lips moved together slowly as he held her tighter against him. As the kiss ended, she turned back towards the stream of light, reaching her hand back out.

"I'm currently enjoying the privilege of not turning into a pile of ash, how are you?" She showed off her sun-bathed hand as Giles continued to hold her.

"I couldn't be better. Not after yesterday."

"Are you referring to the bountiful harvest we ordered for dinner or the copious amounts of sex?" Jenny teased as she cocked her head, staring back at him, replacing her hand from the beam back on his arms.

Giles laughed breathlessly into her hair. "The latter, I am certain," he replied softly, but then he quickly lifted his head.

"However, I was quite surprised with how excellent the banoffee pie was from…from…well, from one of the restaurants," Jenny could see Rupert mentally scanning for the name of the ice cream restaurant they had ordered from.

"Sunnydale Ice Cream and Shakes," Jenny offered.

"Ah, yes. How could I forget a name as clever as that?"

"I think it's because there were way more memorable things from last night, re: the copious amounts of sex. Speaking of, did I remember to tell you how great it was? I mean, being together for about a year without actually….being together, could lead to some very unrealistic expectations for the bedroom. Yet, here we are, in the land of expectations met. Nay exceeded."

"I could say the same of you, darling. And yes, I do believe you mentioned your…satisfaction, on multiple occasions. Though you may have not used those exact words, or words at all, if I recall correctly," he used his teeth to pull the collar of her top back exposing her shoulder, giving it an open mouth kiss.

Jenny threw her head back and cackled with delight, "Wow! 'Smug about Sex' was definitely not on my 'Snobby Rupert" bingo card!"

Giles continued to kiss along her shoulder, whispering against her skin, "If anyone here should be smug, it's you, my love," he brought his mouth to her ear as he continued, "last night…was incredible. Perfect."

"I know what you mean," she responded, leaning into his face.

With a final kiss to her cheek, Rupert moved his head up so he could prop it on her shoulder and ask, "What would you like to do today? We could go to the Espresso Pump for tea and breakfast, possibly talk for a walk in Weatherly Park…I imagine you would enjoy spending today in the sunlight."

"Well, that's partially true. The problem with leaving the house though is that I can't have you naked," Jenny leaned into his chest, wishing she never bothered to do his pajama top.

"Well then, I believe I can propose a reasonable compromise," he said as he pushed them forward closer to the couch, both giggling, so that the beam of light shined brightly on Jenny's face, down her neck, across her chest, and to her stomach before hitting the couch. Rupert reached up and began to unbutton the pajama top as he kissed the back of her neck. Jenny's eyes fluttered closed as she focused on the warmth from the sun and Rupert's soft lips.

"I like the way you think," she whispered as he finished the last button. He moved to pull the top down and off of her shoulders. As it hit the floor, she reached up to circle his head with her arm, the other moving to brace herself against the couch. She craned her neck back and kissed him deeply.

Rupert felt like he was in a dream as if the last 14 hours or so happened outside of reality. His Jenny was here, alive in his arms, molding her body to his, all thoughts of having to stop before passion took over completely driven from his mind. The ache of having her, holding her, loving her, but never being able to make love to her was nothing more than a distant memory now. When she craned her neck back to kiss him, her lips crashing against his without hesitation, he was reminded this was real. Jenny is alive. They're in love.

They no longer needed to worry about being happy.

"God, I want you, babe," Jenny whispered hoarsely as she pulled him against her.

"H-here?" He asked with anticipation buried in a shallow breath, as though he dared to wish for the answer.

"Yes!" She pleaded as she began to grind back against him, desperate to relieve some of the desire coursing through her. Giles groaned in response, burying his face in her hair, meeting her hips with every move.

She moved her hand from his head to grab the waistband of his pajama pants, clumsily starting to push them down. When she couldn't quite get them over his hips, he reluctantly let her go to fully remove them, leaving them both naked, warm to the touch from the sun and their rising heartbeats. He reached back for her, holding her against him.

"Have you any idea what yesterday means to me?" Rupert questioned into her hair breathlessly, one hand gripping her breast and the other making its way between her legs.

"Baby, I do," she gasped as his fingers reached her core and began to slowly rub. She moaned, giving in to the pleasure for a bit, enjoying Rupert's dexterous hands. But she needed to tell him. Even after all of this time, even after becoming a vampire, even after getting her soul back…it was still difficult for her to say to Rupert how much he meant to her. They both knew how the other felt, but for Jenny, saying it too often only solidified how much she needed Rupert – which meant she was vulnerable to a significant loss. But yesterday, something changed. Jenny wasn't typically too sentimental about going to bed with someone, but nothing between her and Rupert had ever been typical, most certainly in their sex life.

Jenny slowly spun around so that she and Rupert were face to face, his hardness pressing against her abdomen, her back against the couch. He gripped her hips against him as she wrapped her arms around his neck. Rupert leaned down to rest his forehead against hers, letting out a long breath.

"Rupert, today…yesterday…all the days before that, they're everything to me," she looked deep into his eyes. "You're everything to me," she whispered, almost scared to say it too loudly.

A grin slowly emerged on Giles' face, that toothy grin that always looks a little bigger than expected, uninhibited with responsibility. A grin typically only reserved for her.

"I adore you, love," he spoke softly but assuredly. His face became more intense as he leaned down to brush her lips with his. "I choose you. You're my destiny."

He held her gaze, searching her eyes. Jenny pulled her arms back so that she could cup his face. Each of their lives had been ruled by a nameless power calling the shots, tugging the strings, and controlling their lives. Destiny and duty and responsibility were to drive them both, not passion, and certainly not for each other. But Jenny understood exactly what Rupert meant.

Let the gods and the demons and the powers-of-whatever fate Jenny and Rupert each be shackled to their own destiny serving a so-called greater purpose. Nothing they preordained could ever be more important than the fact that Jenny and Rupert chose each other.

She looked at him deeply before pulling him into a kiss, sealing that promise.

Rupert started kissing his way down her throat, her neck, her breasts, and her stomach. She sighed, tipped her head back, and let her hands fall to his head. He was on his knees gently pushing her forward so she was flush with the couch. She responded by pushing herself up to sit on the back of it. Before she had time to look down, Rupert had grabbed one of her legs, propping it on his shoulder. Without a word, he buried his tongue in her.

The tension that had been building since he first put his arms around her snapped. Jenny immediately responded by moaning and fisting her hands in his hair tighter. He gently alternated between licking her, burrowing his tongue inside of her, and kissing his way to her clit – all of the motions she seemed to have enjoyed the most from the previous evening. The night before, he obsessively cataloged any action on his part that made her moan or sigh with pleasure. Rupert was eager to discover what exactly made Jenny Calendar fall apart in bed. Their night ended with him having a range of new knowledge he looked forward to putting into action again soon.

She craned her neck as she felt the heat from the sun on her back, mixing into delicious tension as the pleasure built in her core. Rupert looked up and saw Jenny bathed in sunlight, eyes closed, a smile on her face, gasping for air. He alone bore witness to seeing her in the throes of passion. He slowly tongued her clit and held her legs as they began to shake.

She could feel herself reaching a plateau. She left one hand curled in a death grip in his hair as the other reached to clasp the couch. She chanted his name over and over. Rupert responded immediately by speeding up his tongue, refusing to stop.

Finally, she seized, an orgasm exploding inside of her. She felt it racing through her body like electricity. She gasped loudly, letting out a long moan as Rupert used his tongue to guide her through.

Breaking around him, gasping for breath, she gently removed her leg from his shoulder and pulled him up to meet her face. Desperately kissing him, he tasted sweet and musky.

"I love you," he managed to whisper between kisses. "I've wanted this, I've wanted you for so long, and I love you," he moved to kiss her neck and shoulders. She lifted his head to capture his lips in another searing kiss.

"I know, Rupert. I've wanted you for so long. And now," she said with a shaky voice, her mouth curling into a wicked grin, "I can have you."

She quickly twisted herself so that she was facing the couch again, pushing her back into his embrace as the fully risen sun shined bright against her. Rupert leaned in, gripping the back of the couch, an arm on either side of her, his erection pressed against her backside. He kissed along her back, trailing heat from her shoulders down her shoulder blades.

"I need you inside me," she managed to get out before craning her neck back to kiss him. He lifted himself back up to meet her. She moved her legs and raised her hips, letting his cock slip between her legs, finding the wetness of her folds. He moaned against her mouth, breaking the kiss to let out a deep growl from his chest, moving his hips.

"Yes," he whispered hoarsely with shallow breath. He leaned back and held her hips as she braced herself against the couch. He quickly reached over to the desk, pushing papers and mail to find a sleeve of condoms. During their first time the previous evening, Rupert had frustratingly torn open the pack near the loft balcony after several minutes of trying to open it with some finesse. Several of the sleeves exploded over the railing falling downstairs. When they had made their way downstairs to order dinner, he had noted one of the sleeves fell on the desk.

He opened the foil packet and rolled the condom on as fast as he could. It took all of his concentration to focus his attention on the task at hand and not how Jenny currently looked standing in front of him.

Once the condom was on, he reached back for her, lining himself up with her opening. He let his hands trail his fingers lightly down her back from shoulders to her rear, watching her shiver.

Impatiently, Jenny pushed her hips back. Rupert immediately responded by steadying her hips and gently pushing himself inside of her, savoring every moment.

When he was inside of her completely, Jenny groaned and threw her head forward with pleasure.

With Rupert inside of her and the sun cascading around them, she felt like they had built their own reality here. Safe, warm, and buzzing with life and love.

Rupert pulled himself out of her almost completely before pushing all the way back in again, letting out a heavy breath. He continued these movements as he let out a subdued moan. He set the pace, not fast, but relentlessly steady, leaving no room for thought or want.

Jenny felt freer than she ever had. Unashamedly naked, Rupert behind her holding her steady, moving inside of her, sun and warmth and love and pleasure overwhelming her senses. She was lost in him.

Rupert savored the short moan Jenny let escape with every stroke, watching her shudder. He moved one hand from her hip to wrap an arm around her waist as his other hand moved to creep between her legs, finding that bundle of nerves and slowly rubbing as he pulled them closer.

"Oh, Jenny," he whispered coarsely into her ear, speeding up his thrusts, losing himself inside of her, guided by need and feel, held in balance only by his tight grasp on her body.

"Fuck, Rupert," Jenny gasped as she leaned her head back against his shoulder, "you feel so," she couldn't finish her thought as he built her closer and closer to another orgasm. She gripped the back of the couch tighter as her breath became thinner.

He wanted to make her come, he wanted to make her lose herself in sensation, he wanted to make her feel happy and light and in love. He wanted to make her shine.

Jenny let out a loud moan as another orgasm ripped its way through her body. He continued pumping into her, magnifying the intensity of her orgasm with each thrust. She quickly reached down to grab his wrist, halting his fingers on her clit. As he felt her body relax and she let go of his wrist, he gently guided her hands to reach up and circle his head on her shoulder, allowing her to arch her back to mold herself against him completely. Rupert reached up with both hands, each capturing a breast, and sped up his persistent pace. In this position, Jenny couldn't meet him thrust for thrust, and resigned herself to keeping her body steady against him, letting Rupert take control, take her completely.

Moving together, holding unto only each other, clutching desperately and entirely. They were one, and nothing would come between them ever again.

"I'm close," Rupert whispered deep in her ear.

"Yes, please, please come inside me," Jenny gasped, moving one hand to cover his on her breast.

Upon hearing her response, any shred of control he had was lost. He moaned, driving in and out of her. He kissed her ear, her hair, her temple, her neck, her shoulder. Wherever he could reach.

Jenny moaned every time he buried himself within her, repeatedly whispering his name as he pushed her down unto him with each thrust, penetrating her that much more deeply.

Just when he thought he couldn't take any more, his breath caught as he came, stilling inside of her, holding her tightly against him. He was sure he would have lost control of his legs and collapse if Jenny wasn't there steadying them both.

Jenny gripped him even tighter as she felt him come into her. Tried to memorize every gasp and moan as he shook, dizzy with pleasure. Being unable to have sex was not only frustrating because her own sexual needs were left unattended, but because she desperately wanted to be the one to make sure Rupert's were being met. She wanted to know what made him moan and tremble, to be the sole witness to watching Rupert come apart. In that moment, Jenny smiled feeling Giles' powerful grip on her body, his legs shake as she reached out to grip the couch to steady them, feeling and hearing his breathing start to come back to normal as he returned to himself. She swore she would never take this for granted.

Rupert placed one last kiss on her shoulder before releasing his grip on her. Jenny instinctively reared her head back and kissed him. He moved a hand up to caress her face as his tongue slipped into her mouth. The feeling of sweat between them, red marks on their skin from clutching each other in wordless ecstasy, the echoes of their orgasms still making their way through their bodies…all of it, Rupert thought, was perfect.

"God, I can't remember the last time I was this happy," Jenny said softly as their kiss ended. Rupert continued to caress her face.

"I certainly cannot either," Rupert responded breathy, reluctant to let her go. "I can remember you months ago suggesting we might be able to make love without you losing your soul. If the past day proves anything, is that I was certainly right to put a stop to that." Jenny giggled and began to remove herself from Rupert's embrace.

"Well, in my defense, if I recall correctly, I had just walked in on you undressing for a shower. You can't blame me for what I say when you're naked. That's just, not fair."

"Even so," Rupert chuckled, gently removing himself from her and pulling several tissues from the box on his desk, handing some to Jenny. "I think this might be a rare occurrence where I have proven you wrong, dear." Jenny stopped for a second to consider this.

"Fine, but don't let it go to your head, snobby," Jenny finished cleaning herself up, tossing the tissues in the waste bin and putting Rupert's pajama shirt back on, not bothering to button the buttons.

"Speaking of showering, care to join me?" Rupert asked removing and tossing out the condom and pulling his pajama pants back on. "If we are to do, well, anything else today. I am first in desperate need of a shower." Rupert offered, pulling her back into his arms, resting his head on top of her head before depositing a kiss there.

"I like the sound of that," Jenny pulled Rupert against her. As she stood there for a moment in Rupert's arms, enjoying the after-sex bliss, her eyes caught sight of the package from her family, the one containing the pouch of Mohra demon blood. Up until now, she had been successful in simply enjoying the contents of the package without considering why her family had sent it to her to begin with. She looked around and finally spotted the note that came with the pouch; the small, rolled up piece of parchment. It was on the desk, slightly obscured by a Chinese food container that at one point held a pint of orange chicken.

Sensing her distraction, Rupert gently asked, "Everything alright?"

"Yea, yea," she responded distantly. She snapped back to the moment and spoke more assuredly, "Yes. Of course, everything is amazing, I just. This is the first moment I'm really considering how this happened. My family sent me that package. I still haven't read the note."

"Yes, yes, I had thought of that as well," Rupert turned his head to also spot the note on the desk. "Would you like to read it?"

Jenny's mind began to race, a thousand scenarios running through her head. Was the Mohra demon blood meant for her? Was it meant for Angel? What would possess her family to want to cure, not curse, Angel – or herself for that matter. None of it made any sense. Not reading the letter meant she still had some control over the situation, that getting re-ensouled was somehow still on her own terms. But she knew the right thing to do was to know why. She had to know why.

"Yea, I think I do," she stepped away from him and reached for the note.

"Would you like me to stay?" Rupert offered. "I'd, uh, I'd understand if you'd like some privacy-"

"No, I want you to stay, of course." She quickly responded, unspooling the parchment. It felt rough on her fingertips and made a satisfying scratch sound when it rubbed together. Jenny let out a deep breath as she held the note open. Rupert moved to wrap a hand around her waist, tucking her into his side. She immediately recognized the careful handwriting as that of her great uncle.

Janna,

We have tried sending you many letters. We pray this one finally finds you. We have heard what misfortune has fell upon you. No matter what failings you perceive you are responsible for, know that the curse of a soul was never meant for anyone in our family – including you. We've accepted that Angelus' reappearance was fated to pass and there was nothing you could have done to stop it. The family does not blame you. Despite our differences and your choice to stay in America with the slayer, her watcher, and their kin, we would never want one of our own to live a life as a vampire cursed with the pain of remorse. Enclosed is the blood of a Mohra Demon, capable of breathing life back into your body. Please make use of it as soon as possible.

Your family always

Jenny finished reading, letting out an audible sigh in disbelief. She barely registered Rupert's soft, "My god" as she reread the letter. There was nothing you could have done to stop it…the family does not blame you. These were the words she dreamed of hearing from her family. She never thought she'd actually experience reading them.

Jenny began to drop her hands and let out a small laugh. Rupert immediately grabbed the letter from her hands and held it up to his face slowly mouthing the same passages Jenny was fixated on.

"I can't believe this, Rupert," Jenny looked up at her lover, tears in her eyes.

"Nor can I," Rupert responded flipping the back of the letter to see if anything else was included on the note.

"My family doesn't blame me. They've been trying to get

in touch with me. They forgive me."

"Forgive? Jenny, they don't blame you for anything necessitating forgiveness."

Jenny closed her eyes tightly, tears spilling unto her cheeks.

"Oh, darling, it's alright," Rupert spoke comfortingly, wiping away her tears with his thumbs.

"Ugh, I know. It's just, it's just been an emotional weekend," she let out a small laugh, causing Giles to softly chuckle. He moved to put the letter back on the table before reaching up to cup her face.

"It has indeed," Rupert offered. "I am so thankful they reached out. I feel, err, well, I am very sorry for the things I have said about them in the past." Rupert shifted his gaze, clearly remorseful for his actions.

"I appreciate that, thank you. For what it is worth, I can see your side. I don't think I'd ever be able to say something nice about your father," Jenny offered, remembering all of the terrible things Rupert has told her about the Giles patriarch.

"Well, lucky for us, I am not inclined to ever ask for that," Rupert replied quickly. "Perhaps you can write back? Or at least read the rest of the correspondence they've sent this past year?"

"Yea, that sounds like a good plan. Sending a letter back is a must. But first, I think I want to enjoy the day together before we have to deal with, you know," she gestured at the two of them and all of the take-out boxes. "We have so much to figure out! God, we have to tell the kids! I wonder if I could get my old job back. We could just tell Snyder I decided to move back to Sunnydale."

"Given Snyder still has Willow teaching your classes, I would venture to guess you'd be welcomed back with open arms. But first, I agree, let's spend today together. We'll manage the reality of the last day or so tomorrow," Rupert placed a kiss on her head, pausing to gauge her reaction.

"Sounds perfect. Now, I believe you mentioned something of a shower," Jenny leaned into him teasingly.

"Yes, first item on the to do list."

"Well, I think I was the first item on your to do list."

Rupert groaned, "Oh, don't tell me that's revenge for the satisfaction comment earlier."

"Listen, in the immortal words of the Spice Girls, 'If you want to be my lover, you gotta be okay with me making corny jokes about us doing it.'"

"I'm fairly confident that is not the lyric."

"How would you know?"

"Well, er, I simply hope it isn't. I would hate to think that's the music Buffy is listening to."

Jenny let out a powerful laugh, wriggling out of Rupert's embrace heading towards the shower. She reached back to grab his hand.

"Come on, England. We have a day to get started and a life to live." Jenny tugged Rupert's arm until he wordlessly followed her into the bathroom.

All things considered, both Jenny and Rupert couldn't wait to get started on both, together.

Epilogue; Hope

Rupert always loved the sound of his heels clicking against the hallways of Sunnydale High at night. The steady pace, the rhythmic clunk, the slight echo off of the walls. It was pleasant. It meant there were no other students around and he could have a moment of solitude. He thought maybe he should find the darkened hall sinister or at least foreboding – an empty school always feels a bit out of sorts as it is – but he found it quite comforting. Almost as if time had paused and he could take a moment to relax, the darkness blanketed his worry in a way.

And if he were truly honest with himself, he'd admit that walking these halls after hours reminded him of the many times he did this walk after hours on the way to see his girlfriend. Over winter, the sun would set shortly after the students were dismissed and that meant stolen time could be found in her classroom. He smiled at the memories, but they faded when he reminded himself that he and that girlfriend were still estranged, torn apart by the revelation of why she was really in Sunnydale. He wished he could pretend this was just another winter walk to see her, uncomplicated by truths uncovered and duties revealed.

As he continued through the silent halls on the way to his car, he stopped when his eyes caught the light coming from her classroom down the hall to the right. Not bright enough to be the main lights, but just dim and focused enough to be her computer monitor. A soft smile involuntarily appeared on his face. He stood there for a moment considering his options before turning the corner away from the direct path to his car and towards her classroom.

They spoke for the first time yesterday. In her classroom after Willow disappeared with a still upset Buffy. He had hoped for a possible reconciliation between the two women, but Buffy clearly still blamed Jenny for keeping her connection with Angel a secret. He knew that unless Buffy could forgive her, or at least not outright see her as an enemy, there was no chance for him and Jenny to, well, do anything.

And then she admitted that she loved him.

Rupert was stunned. He never dared to believe she felt as deeply for him as he had for her. When they rekindled their romance after Eyghon, Rupert knew he was in love with her. That he wanted to be with her and she made him happier than he thought he would ever deserve. But he could never quite get himself to believe she loved him back. He knew she cared for him, of course, but he did not want to test his luck. Finding someone he loved as much as Jenny was rare enough, her loving him back in earnest was entirely impossible.

He replayed her words in his head as he approached her door. I didn't know I was gonna fall in love with you. If fate was kind enough to have Jenny Calendar fall in love with him, maybe it was kind enough to have Buffy Summers forgive her.

When he reached her classroom, he stood in the door frame for a moment, admiring her in her element. For all of the grief, he would give her about computers, he couldn't help but be charmed when he'd find her deep in thought provoked by something on that blasted screen. Something on that blasted screen had clearly inspired such deep thought now.

Giles noted the mug of coffee next to her. She's going to be up all night, she knows that he thought disapprovingly.

"Hello," he spoke timidly, reluctant to disturb her.

She was startled a bit as she quickly turned around to see him.

"Oh, hi!" She swiftly turned back, typing something into the computer to make whatever she was reading disappear.

"You're working late," Giles offered as he tentatively entered her classroom.

"Special project," she replied, looking happy to be speaking with him.

"Oh," Giles responded. He thought to ask her more about it when she interrupted.

"I spoke to Buffy today."

All thoughts of the project left his brain immediately as he more assuredly walked towards her, sitting next to her on her desk. Not touching her, but closer to her than he had been in weeks. It felt right.

She picked up a pencil, eyeing it, and spoke with that familiar teasing nature, "She said you missed me."

Giles looked down, abashed. It was bad enough that Buffy and the children got involved in his personal affairs, it was entirely cruel that they tended to have an accurate assessment of them. However, he couldn't help but think that Buffy revealing this information to Jenny must have meant she was okay with him missing her too.

"Yes, well, she's…a meddlesome girl."

"Rupert," Jenny started. He slowly looked up at her. It had been weeks since someone used his first name. He was Giles when he was a Watcher and Mr. Giles when he was a librarian. He only got to be Rupert with her.

"Okay, I don't wanna say anything if I'm wrong, but I may have some news. Now, I need to finish up here. Could I see you later?" She asked with a mix of uncertainty and hope.

"Y-yes, yes," and before he could stop himself, he finished, "you could stop by my house." He hoped she picked up on the intimate nature of the suggestion. Not that he was implying that…well, anything would happen later, but one does not typically extend a late-night invitation to one's home to just a colleague, let alone an enemy.

A genuine smile crept across her face, "Okay."

"Good," he replied, now sporting a full-on grin. He thought than to get up and leave her to her work, but something was holding him there. He continued staring at her. His smile faded as his face got more serious.

"I have missed you," he admitted.

Her grin remained intact, though much softer now than teasing. She slowly moved her hand to cover his on the desk.

"I've missed you too," she said quietly, practically in a whisper. "We can talk later? About all of it?" She gave his hand a gentle squeeze. He continued looking at her intensely as if he were frozen, unable to respond now that she was touching him again. As if he did not have the willpower to break their connection now that she made it.

"Hey," she said with a smile. "it's all gonna be okay. Eventually. I can tell," she gave his hand another small squeeze.

He knew how screwed up everything was. He knew how many lies they had told each other. He knew that in some sense they were destined to be enemies. He knew how hopeless the situation was with Angelus on the loose. But he couldn't help himself, because, at that moment when he looked at her when he felt her hand on his, all he felt was hope.

Because even with all things considered, he believed her.

* 9 7 8 9 3 5 6 6 7 1 3 6 2 *